# NEW SHOES

# CHRIS RASCHKA

GREENWILLOW BOOKS, AN IMPRINT OF HARPERCOLLINS PUBLISHERS

New Shoes
Copyright © 2018 by Chris Raschka
All rights reserved. Printed in the
United States of America. For information
address HarperCollins Children's Books,
a division of HarperCollins Publishers,
195 Broadway, New York, NY 10007.
www.harpercollinschildrens.com

Watercolor and gouache paint on paper
were used to prepare the full-color art.
The text type is Futura Bold.

Library of Congress
Cataloging-in-Publication Data
is available.
ISBN 978-0-06-265752-7
(hardback)

18  19  20  21  PC
10  9  8  7  6  5  4  3  2

First Edition
Greenwillow Books

To Keith

# Mommy is going to put my shoes on me.

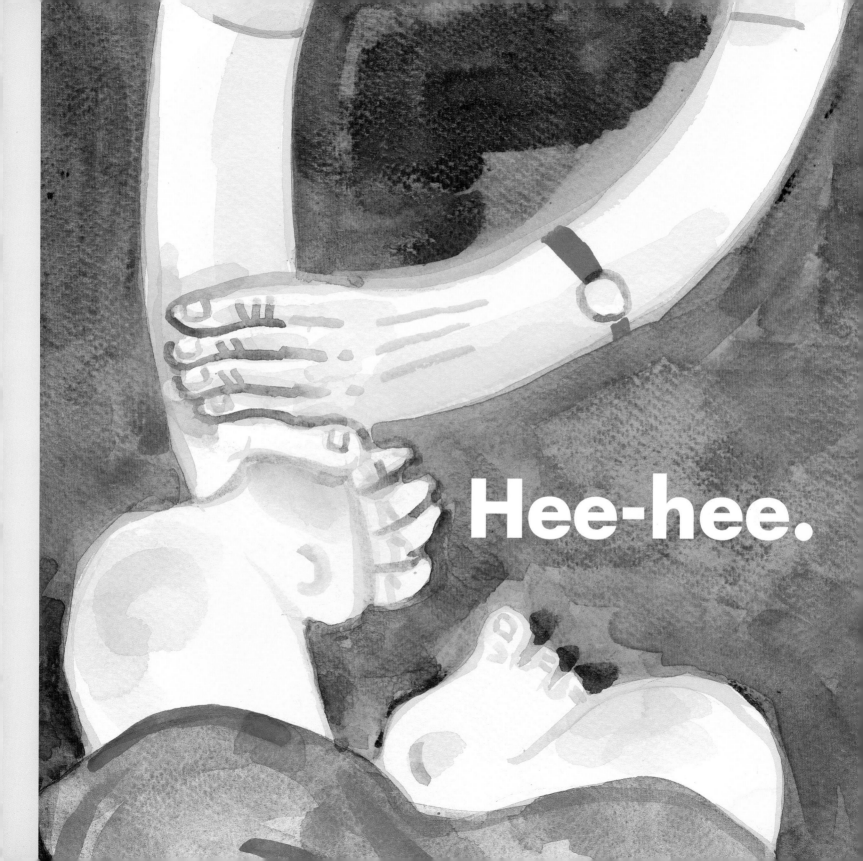

Mommy
puts on
my
socks.

Mommy puts on my old shoes.

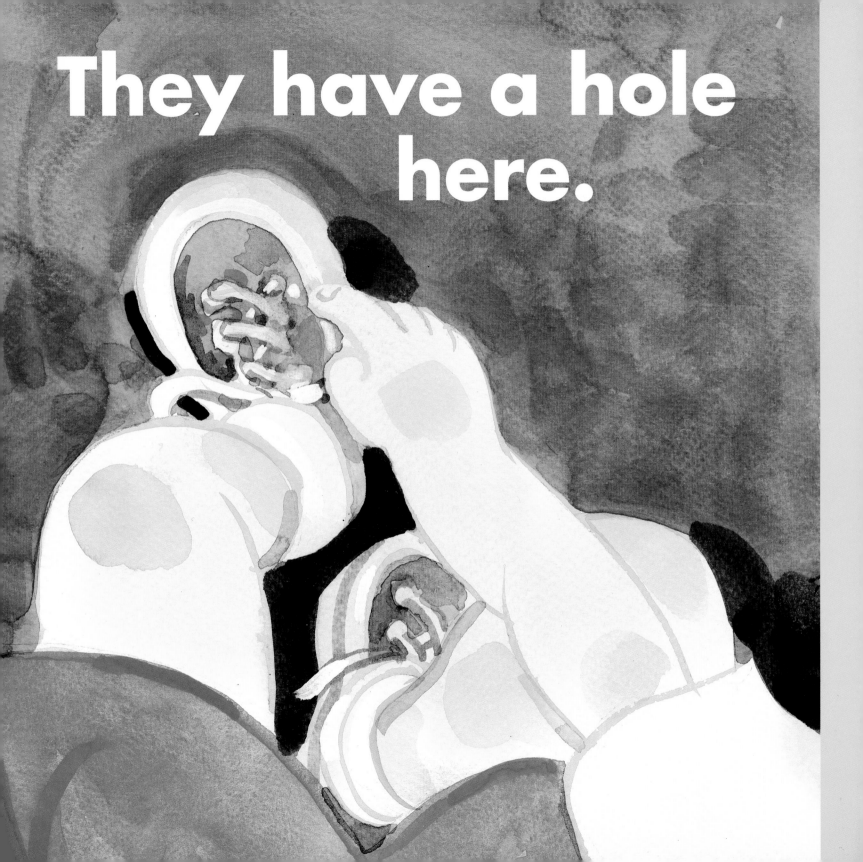

And a hole here.

I can put
my finger in.
Hee-hee!

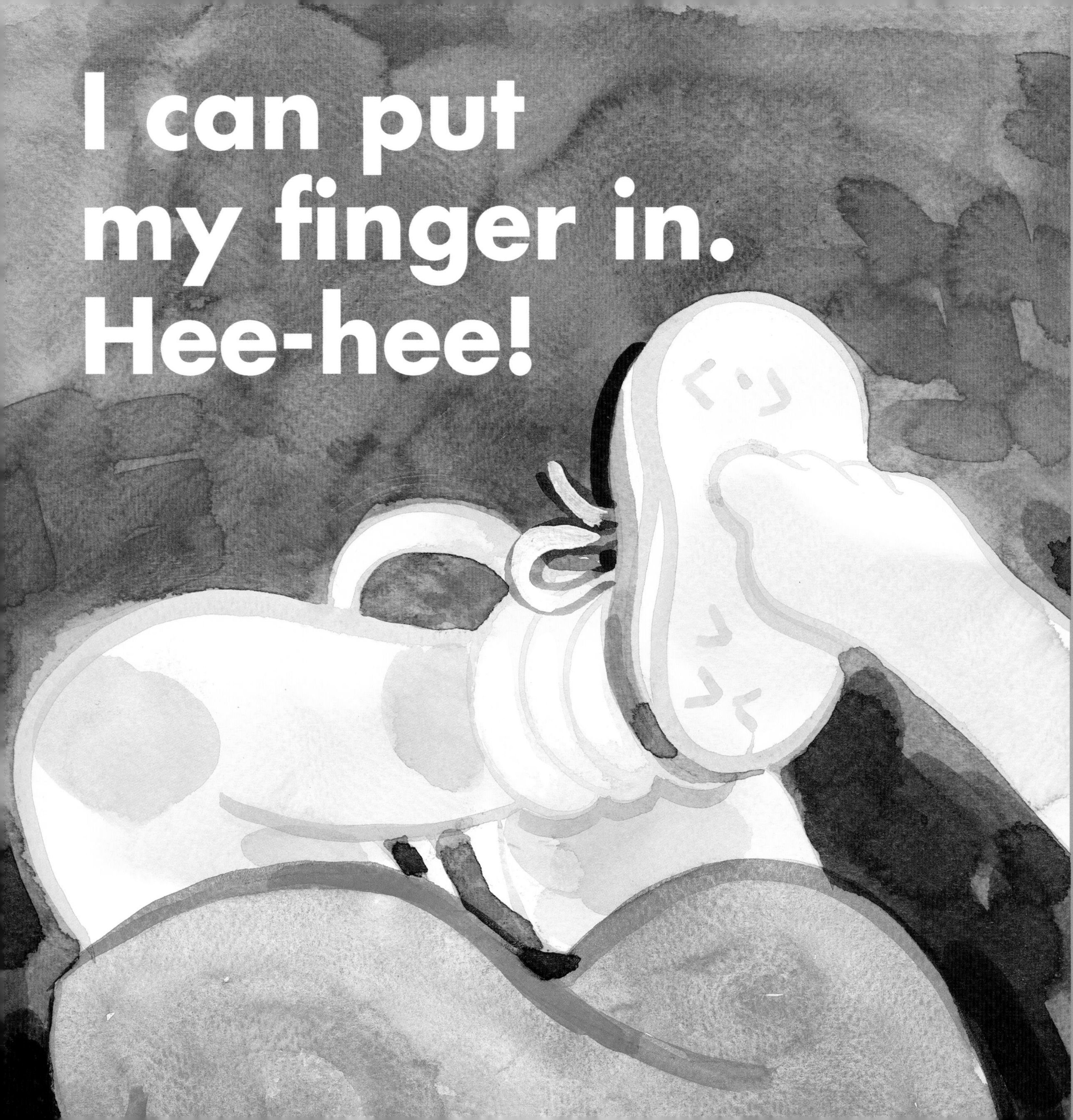

Dirt could get in.
Or water.

Let's go to the shoe store.

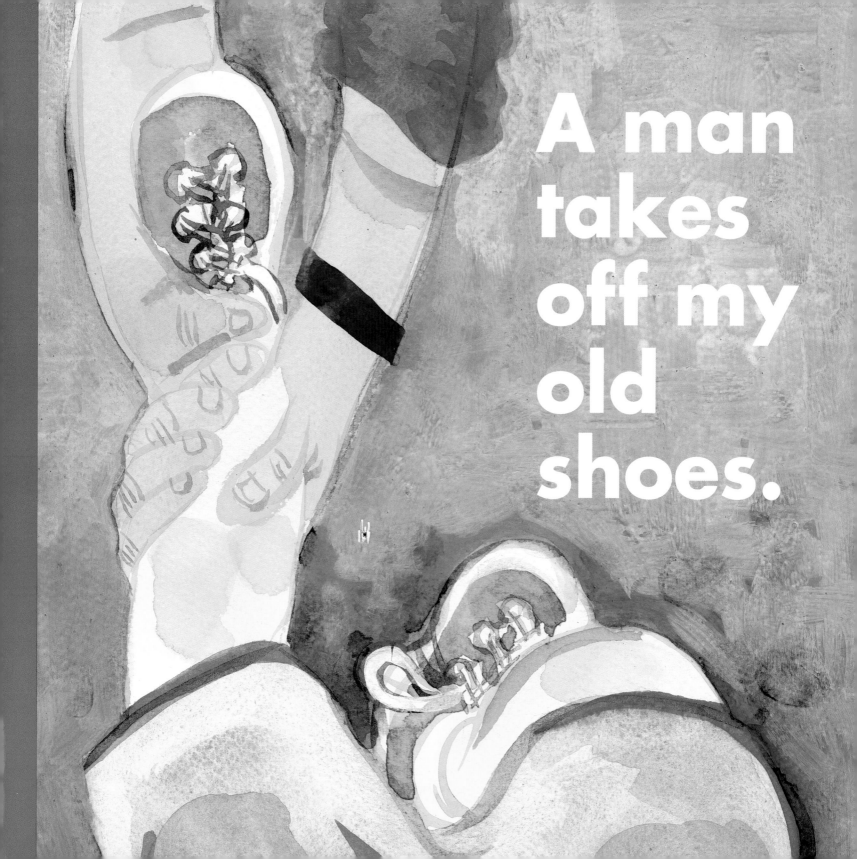

A man takes off my old shoes.

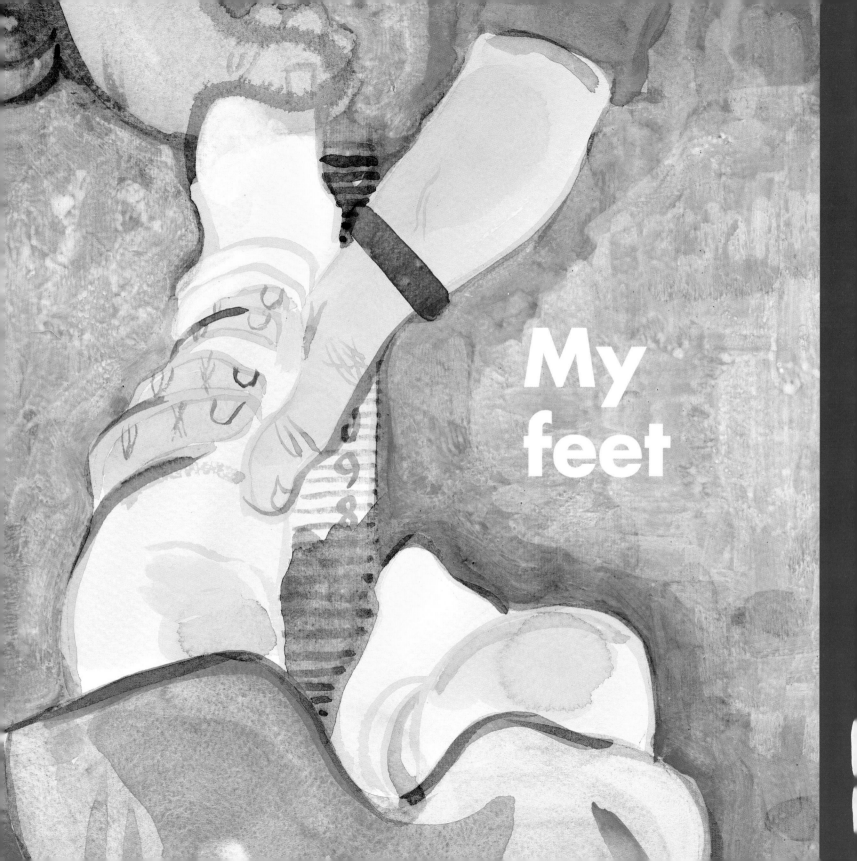

My
feet

are
bigger
than
before!

# Now to choose new shoes.

# I like these.

And
I like those.

They are a little pinchy right there.

# and outside.

I
can
run

in
my
new
shoes!

I want
to show
Emma.

I love my

new shoes!